Littleland

All Day Long

First published 2013 by Nosy Crow Ltd
The Crow's Nest, 10a Lant Street
London SE1 1QR
www.nosycrow.com

This edition first published 2014
ISBN 978 0 85763 148 0

A CIP catalogue record for this book is available from the British Library.

Printed in China

Papers used by Nosy Crow are made from wood
grown in sustainable forests.

1 3 5 7 9 8 6 4 2

Littleland
All Day Long

Marion Billet

Hello and welcome to Littleland!

Can you see...?

flower

ball

bird

sun

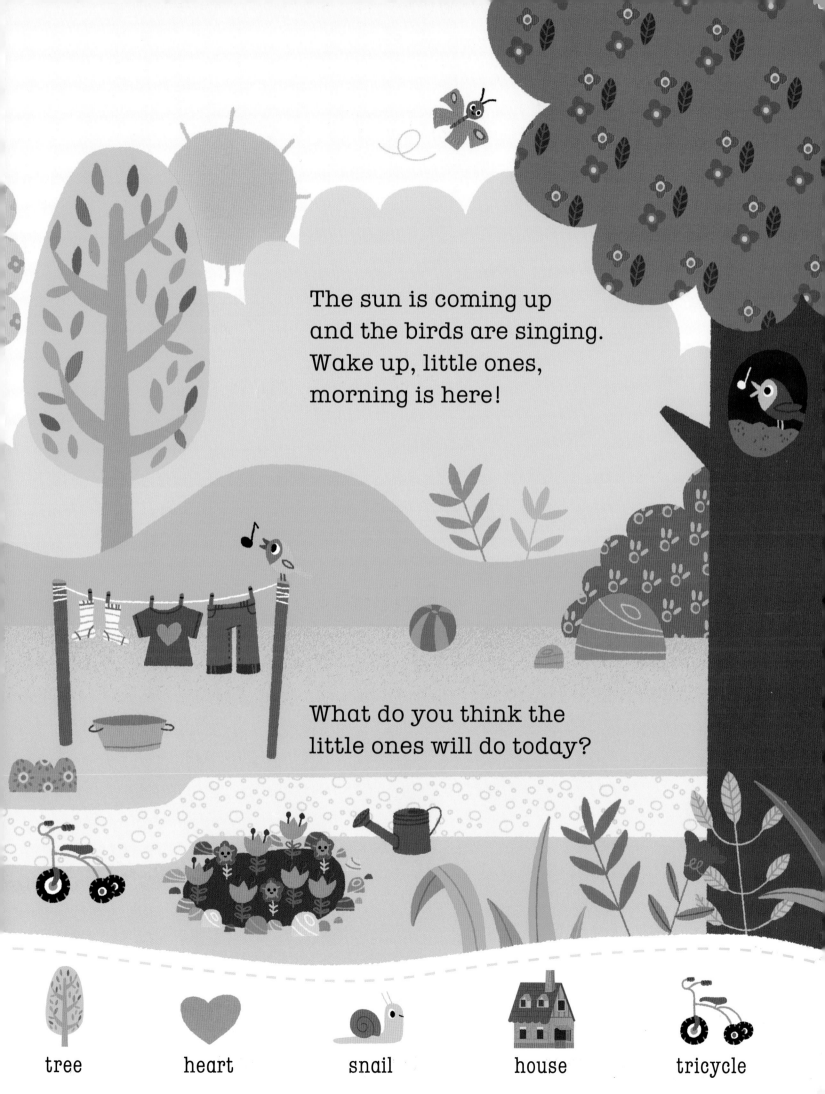

The sun is coming up
and the birds are singing.
Wake up, little ones,
morning is here!

What do you think the
little ones will do today?

tree   heart   snail   house   tricycle

First, the little ones need to get dressed. But little Koala has lost a sock! Can you see where it is?

Can you see...?

chair

train

telephone

drum

Their bedroom is a tiny
bit messy, isn't it?
Is your room ever untidy?

teddy   shoe   dinosaur   T-shirt   bed

The little ones are feeling very hungry!
They can't wait to eat their breakfast.

Have you noticed
that they all like to
eat different things?

Can you
see...?

saucepan

bowl

glass

spoon

What did you have
for breakfast today?
Was it yummy?

milk   jam   key   picture   stool

It's time to play in the garden. The little ones are swinging, sliding and making lots of noise, too!

What do you like to do outside?

Can you see...?

squirrel   hat   rabbit   pushchair

Uh-oh! Someone's getting very muddy. Can you see who it is?

wheelbarrow bucket watering can monkey spade

The little ones have come to the town to do their shopping. What a busy place it is.

TOYS

cafe

Be careful crossing the road, little ones, don't forget to hold hands!

Can you see...?

lion

apple

basket

window

BOOKSHOP

fruit

balloon   pigeon   fish   aeroplane   lamp

The little ones are at the supermarket now. Everyone helps out so it doesn't take long to get the things they need.

Oranges

Carrots

Tomatoes

Can you see...?

money

bananas

orange

till

That's a very full trolley, isn't it?
Perhaps it's time to stop shopping
now, little Bear?

trolley   carrot   biscuits   purse   bottle

The shopping is finally finished so now the little ones can have a picnic in the park. They are very happy. Hooray!

Can you see...?

ladybird

cheese

plate

grapes

But, oh dear, somebody is sad.
Poor little Dog, did you bump
your knee?

butterfly   tomato   bee   pear   kite

The little ones have come to help
out on the farm this afternoon.
Everyone has a different job to do.
It's hard work getting everything done!

How many piglets
can you count?

Can you
see...?

cow   chick   brush   ladder

Do you know what noises the farm animals make?

pig   eggs   sheep   tractor   tap

What a busy day it's been for the little ones! They're looking forward to getting home now. Lots of other people are driving home too, aren't they?

Can you see...?

lorry

motorbike

helmet

boat

How do you get home
to your house?

 helicopter

wheel

car

bicycle

bus

Home at last. The little ones have had their supper and now it's bathtime. They like to play in the bubbles with their toys.

Can you see...?

shampoo

potty

soap

bath

Little Lamb is doing very good brushing indeed! Who is feeling most tired, do you think?

towel

loo roll

hairbrush

duck

toothbrush

At the end of the day, the little ones love to read books in their cosy chair. There's just time for one last story before they go to bed.

How many books have the little ones read tonight?

Can you see...?

curtains   slippers   pillow   book

But someone is
asleep already.
Shh, don't wake him!

mobile   rug   blanket   light   clock

Night has fallen and all is quiet in Littleland. Good night, little ones!

Can you see...?

bat   hedgehog   star   fox

Good night, moon.
Good night, stars.
And good night, Littleland.
See you again soon!

owl
nest
mouse
moon
mushroom